What people are saying about …

COTTONMOUTH AND THE GREAT GIFT

"Profoundly written and beautifully illustrated, C. S. Fritz's *Cottonmouth and the Great Gift* reminds us that the kingdom of God comes to those who receive it like children. This is a moving parable of grace and redemption."

Mike Erre, pastor and author of *Astonished*

"Casey has presented the gospel story in such a poignant, unexpected package, our family can't help but read it over and over again. Not only does our six-year-old son, James, sit in rapt attention to the story of Frederick and Tug and the cast of vivid characters, but we wiped away bittersweet tears, finding our own story of loss and redemption in these pages as we seek to answer the question: 'What do we do with the unexpected gift of our pain?' Thank you, Casey, for creating a modern allegory reflecting all our journeys, one that doesn't shy away from the gray storm clouds or deep holes of life but simultaneously strains toward the hopeful light breaking through them."

Jay and Katherine Wolf, founders of Hope Heals, www.hopeheals.com

"Casey Fritz has done it again. His enchanting illustrations, magnificent story telling, and loveable characters make *Cottonmouth and the Great Gift* a delight for both young and old. My daughter and I are eagerly awaiting book three!"

Jessica Thompson, coauthor of *Give Them Grace*

"C. S. Fritz has done it again! With prose that takes you on an adventure and illustrations that stretch the imagination, *Cottonmouth and the Great Gift* will not only grab your attention, it will invigorate your soul. This book causes my children to think about the deeper things of life, and it helps me think like a child again. We love this book."

Jeremy Treat, pastor at Reality LA
and author of *The Crucified King*

COTTONMOUTH AND THE GREAT GIFT
Published by David C Cook
4050 Lee Vance View
Colorado Springs, CO 80918 U.S.A.

David C Cook Distribution Canada
55 Woodslee Avenue, Paris, Ontario, Canada N3L 3E5

David C Cook U.K., Kingsway Communications
Eastbourne, East Sussex BN23 6NT, England

The graphic circle C logo is a registered trademark of David C Cook.

This story is a work of fiction. Characters and events are the product of the author's
imagination. Any resemblance to any person, living or dead, is coincidental.

LCCN 2014944344
ISBN 978-1-4347-0690-4

© 2014 C. S. Fritz
Published in association with the literary agency D. C. Jacobson & Associates LLC,
an Author Management Company. www.dcjacobson.com

The Team: Alex Field, Amy Konyndyk, Ingrid Beck, Karen Athen, Carly Razo
Cover Design: C. S. Fritz
Cover Illustration: C. S. Fritz
Colored by Phil Schorr

Printed in the United States of America

First Edition 2014

1 2 3 4 5 6 7 8 9 10

063014

C. S. FRITZ PRESENTS

COTTONMOUTH
· and the ·
GREAT GIFT

David C Cook®

For Violet—
You are bananas, wild, and bonkers …
don't ever change.

When was the last time you saw a monster?

For little ten-year-old Frederick Cottonmouth, it was mere moments ago. The particular monster Freddie witnessed could only be described as ghastly. Its huge lumpy eyes, its brightly colored fur, and its wings ... its wings were the worst part!

Frederick knew there were monsters of all kinds around him, but none like Tug. As Frederick walked home and turned the dented doorknob to his little home, he couldn't help but think of the love and sacrifice Tug had made for him. It was something Freddie had never experienced before. But now, Tug was gone forever.

It's colder than usual this morning, Freddie thought to himself. It was the kind of morning when the sky slowly turns from white to blue. The kind of morning that starts off cold but will quickly turn warm. *The type of morning to forget one's troubles and go fishing,* Freddie thought.

The floorboards creaked and cracked as Frederick made his way to the closet under the stairs in search of his pole. But just as he reached for the fishing rod, there came a loud thump from upstairs, making the house shake and the windows rattle. Freddie froze in anticipation, staring into the abyss of the upper floor …

Dark brown fur, curly horns, and a plump form filled the dark hallway.

It was Tug!

Tug's smile was so big, Freddie could count every crooked tooth in his oversized mouth.

"Thirty-four," Tug said, knowing Freddie's thoughts.

Frederick's smile turned to laughter as he ran up the wooden stairs and into Tug's giant arms. "I thought I'd lost you, Tug," whispered Frederick, squeezing him tight.

"How could you lose me? I'm huge!" Tug exclaimed, then let out a booming laugh. Though Freddy could have stayed in that moment forever, it didn't last long before Tug grabbed his wrist and moved toward the back door. "Listen, Freddie. There isn't much time!"

Tug led Freddie all the way to the bank of the river, stopped where the water met the shore, then looked to rolling clouds above.

Frederick's nerves began to fade as Tug stood like a mountain with his chin lifted high.

Tug was silent for what felt like many long minutes, and right as Frederick was opening his mouth to break the silence, Tug spoke.

listen very closely

"Frederick. I have to tell you something very important. I need you to do something for me. I need you to go and deliver something to someone who is in grave despair. I don't want you to be naïve, Frederick, this is a dangerous thing I ask of you."

As Tug was explaining Freddie's mission, he slowly reached into the river and pulled out a handful of wet earth.

Like an artist he sculpted the dirt into a small familiar shape. He then wiped the muddy edges exposing a perfect black egg. Freddie immediately took a step back in fear, unwilling to go through that pain again. Sensing this, Tug gently placed the egg in Frederick's hand. "You have no reason to be afraid. We don't have much time, so listen carefully. You must get this egg to the girl with two different colored eyes. She is in The Great Blue."

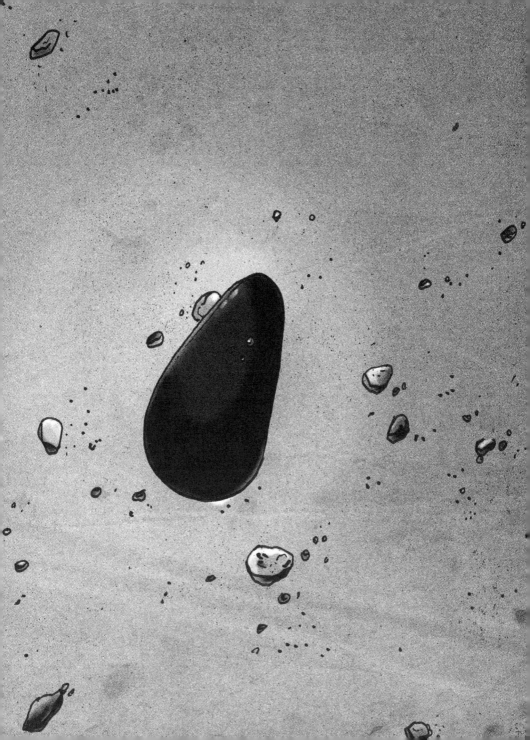

"How will we find her?" Freddie asked.

"Freddie, I must go back," Tug said, placing his big furry hands on Freddie's cheeks.

"Go back? Go back where? I don't want this egg! Can't I just come with you?"

"My dear Frederick … not now, but soon. I promise I will come back for you, but first you must complete this task while I go and prepare a place for you."

Freddie looked down at the river, confused as he remembered his parents' last goodbye. "I have to be alone again?" he asked softly.

Tug smiled and quietly said, "No, Freddie. Not this time. I came to give you a gift. This gift is my prize possession, my treasure, my friend. He will guide you on your mission, Frederick. In the ways I have been there for you, he will be there for you; and in the ways I have comforted you, he will comfort you. He will teach you, and ultimately, he will give you power."

Tug now had Freddie's full attention. His green eyes grew wide with wonder. "Power?"

Tug began to blow into his hands. He made the most beautiful sound, as if all the mighty rushing wind in the forest were flowing through his fingers. All the surrounding pebbles and rocks started to dance and jump with one another, and then the light … *So much light.*

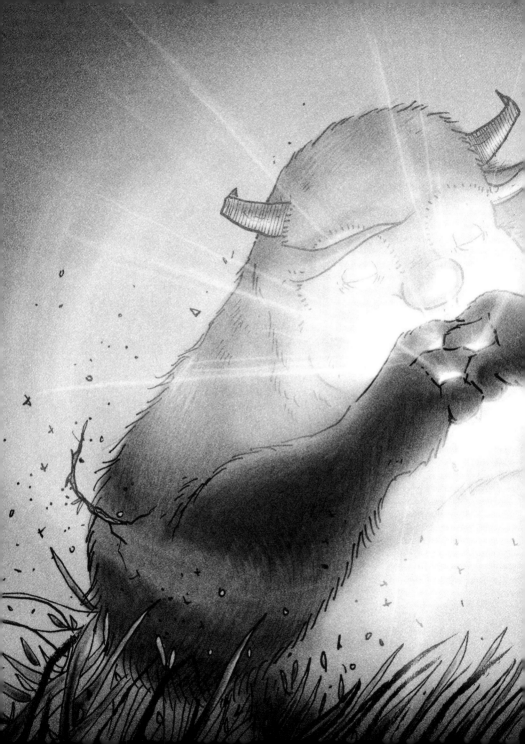

With his hair whipping about his face and struggling to keep his foothold, Frederick stared into the light shooting from Tug's massive hands. The intensity of the light made him feel dizzy and unstable.

Frederick quickly lost his balance as everything around him went …

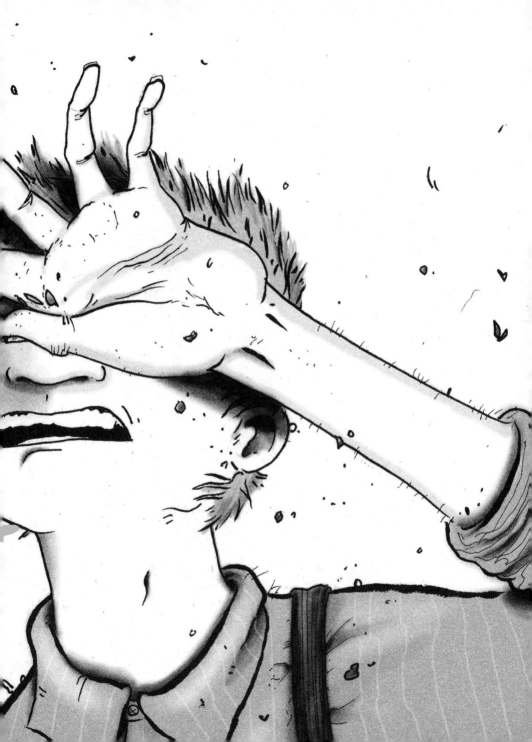

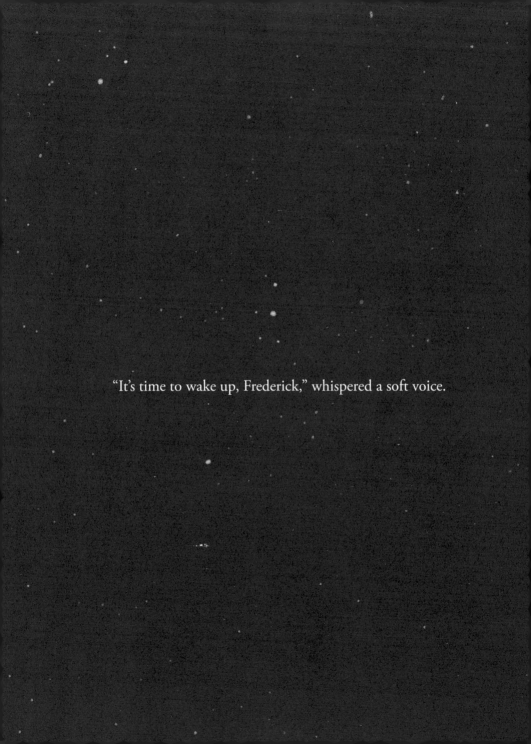

"It's time to wake up, Frederick," whispered a soft voice.

"Mother, is that you?" asked Frederick.

Frederick woke up slowly to see two bright yellow eyes staring at him. "Tug, what happened?" Frederick asked as he rubbed his dry eyes and face. As Frederick sat up, panic sank deep into his heart. Not only did he notice he was far from home, but he also seemed to be far from solid ground. "Tug, where are we?" he asked while frantically scouting out the situation.

Again a still small voice whispered in his ear,

Tug is gone.

Freddie nearly jumped out of the boat when he realized that what he had thought was Tug, was actually something quite different. "What are you?" Freddie yelled, peeking through his dirty fingers.

"Be still. I am known as Yellowthroat, the Gift," the voice said. Frederick noticed that it spoke every word softly and with care, each syllable stretched out like a piece of gum stuck to the bottom of a shoe. Freddie's fear melted away as he realized the voice didn't come from a big monster but from something quite common.

A small bird.

A hummingbird to be exact.

Yellowthroat was beautiful. His feathers were the most perfect black, except for a very small patch of yellow below his slender beak. Yellowthroat's eyes were a shade of golden-yellow identical to Tug's. In fact, Frederick noticed that they were like Tug's eyes in every way but size.

"What are you doing here?" Freddie asked hesitantly.

"I am Tug's gift to you, young Frederick. I am here to—"

"Tug! Where is he?" Freddie asked, interrupting Yellowthroat midsentence.

Yellowthroat responded with a most unfortunate answer. "He is gone, young Frederick. And we have an important job to complete. That is why you are here in this boat … and that is why I am here with you."

Frederick remembering everything Tug had told him, put his chin up and faced the bow. "How long will we be on the river?"

"That is up to the river," Yellowthroat said with great confidence.

"But, it will lead us to The Great Blue, right?" Freddie asked.

"Only one creature knows where The Great Blue is. We must find that creature. We find it; we find the girl with two colored eyes. And so on."

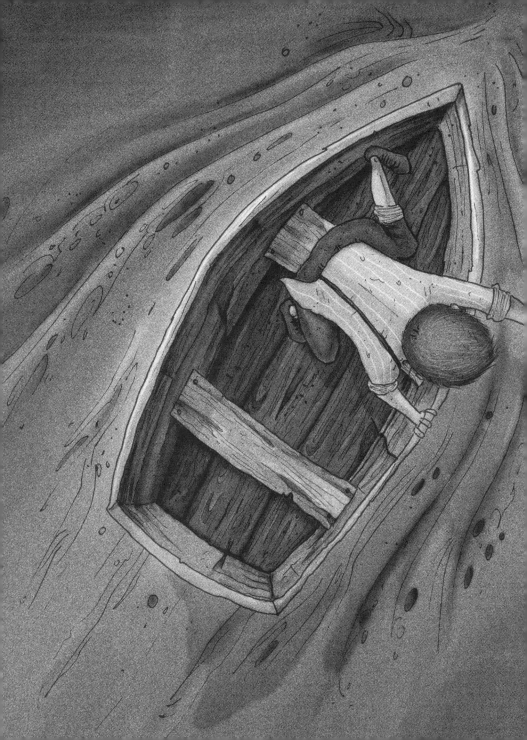

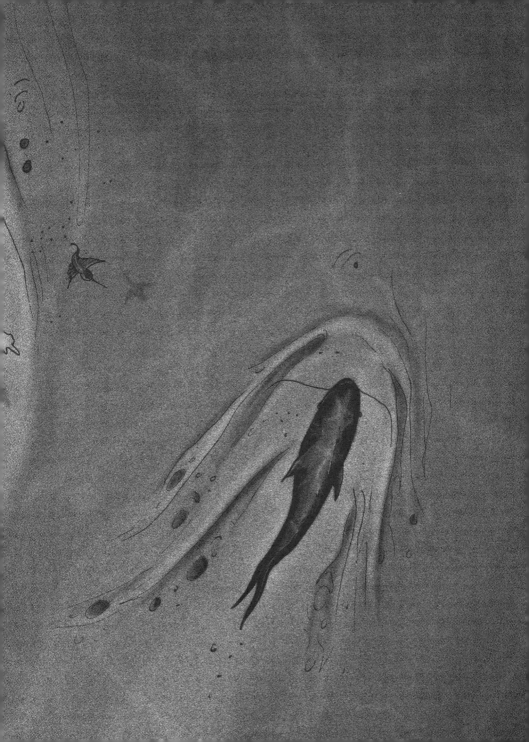

For miles and miles and days and days, they floated, but on one particular day in their journey—a day so humid the air felt thick like soup—the roaring river became quiet and slow. As the boat glided past trees and daffodils, it floated by something unexpected: a bookcase.

And there, in the thick of the forest, stood not just one but more than ten wooden bookcases, overflowing with old hardbound books and ancient scrolls.

"Can we stop the boat and explore, Yellowthroat? I must stretch my legs," Frederick said excitedly.

He hopped into the shallow mossy water and dragged the boat ashore. The two of them moved from book to book, Freddie wiping away cobwebs and dried leaves. As they came upon the last bookcase Freddie could smell a burning candle. Carefully coming closer to the bookcase, they could hear something grumbling. Yellowthroat and Frederick paused and looked at each other with concerned faces.

"Hello, is someone there?" Freddie called out.

The grumbling abruptly stopped.

Silence filled the forest—until it was broken by a loud burp.

Frederick chuckled as Yellowthroat rolled his eyes. To Freddie's surprise, a small troll came out from behind the bookcase. The troll was giggling, with his hand covering his bearded chin.

"Oh, excuse me," the troll said. "I didn't know we had guests."

Frederick had never seen a troll, or even believed in them for that matter. But as Freddie strolled the forest with a talking hummingbird and a magic egg in his back pocket, he felt almost silly for not expecting to discover a troll. This particular troll was wearing a tall crimson hat and had a frizzy gray beard. He had buttons and straps going every which way on his chest and shoulders. He smelled of red maple and jangled as he walked.

Frederick leaned in. "I'm Frederick Cottonmouth, and this is Yellowthroat. What's your name?"

"Yes, who are you and what are you doing here, troll? Do you live here?" Yellowthroat asked.

Ignoring Yellowthroat, the troll came very close to Frederick and looked deeply into his ten-year-old eyes. "You're Cottonface?"

"Cottonmouth," Freddie cheerfully corrected the troll.

"Yeah, sure. Cottonmouth. Well, my name is Gloom and this is Matilda." Gloom held up a water-filled container carelessly strapped to his back. Inside was a large purple and orange octopus. "Isn't she pretty? She's my best friend. Whelp, Cottonfinger, I bet you're here for your gift, aren't you?"

Frederick, shocked by Gloom's question, thought to ask only one thing: "Did Tug give it to you?"

Gloom gave a confirming smirk. "He sure did, didn't he, Matilda? She's shy around people she doesn't know that well. Trust me; she'll loosen up. Then you can't get her to stop gabbing!" Gloom scurried to one of the bookcases stuffed with large books and ran his stubby fingers down the spine of almost every book. "There you are," Gloom whispered as he gingerly removed a heavy book. "Here it is, Cottonnose!" he called.

Freddie eagerly took the book from Gloom and analyzed every detail. "You think it will tell us exactly where The Great Blue is, Yellowthroat?"

Then Freddie opened the hard cover to find a short inscription. He began to read the words aloud while Gloom and Yellowthroat eagerly waited to hear what was written.

"Every day for the past two years, Frederick Cottonmouth had walked to the churning white river near his little home …"

Frederick stopped to make eye contact with Yellowthroat. "Wait… is this book about me?" he asked.

"Go on, go on," Yellowthroat said.

"And every day for the past two years, the river had been a friend to Frederick …"

"I don't understand what I'm reading," Freddie whispered.

"You are reading what you need to read. Tug's words will guide and direct us. We're on the right track, young Frederick. You need to see how your story fits into Tug's story! This book is his story, and it outlines this quest and that our purpose in doing this is all for him."

Freddie turned to the next page and read on.

The book spoke of their great adventures in the deep sea, the times they enjoyed sweet treats, and even mentioned the white rat, Menson. Freddie absorbed every word, reliving his adventure as if for the first time. But what was peculiar about this particular book was its ending. As Freddie continued, he read about Yellowthroat and setting out on the river in the old rickety boat. In fact, the book continued up to the point where Freddie started reading the very book he was holding! As this realization settled in, Freddie read the last line:

"And then Frederick realized this book was more than an ordinary book."

Frederick turned the page. Blank.

Another page. Blank.

He thumbed through all the pages until he reached the last. All blank.

"Well? Where's the ending?" Freddie asked.

"It's not over," Yellowthroat replied with a chuckle. "If anything, we've just begun."

Gloom couldn't help but stare at Freddie. "You don't know, do you?"

"Know what?" Freddie asked. "Where The Great Blue is? No, but the river does."

"Beware, Cotttontoes. Be very aware of deep woodlands in The Great Blue. Something lives in them trees there," Gloom said as he held tight to Frederick's single suspender.

After a moment or two, Freddie finally broke free of Gloom's grip and worriedly walked back toward the boat with the book under his arm.

"One more thing," Gloom yelled and ran toward the boat, "you might need these." He gave Yellowthroat and Freddie a lantern and a satchel full of plums and a butter cake.

"What do you think are in those trees, Yellowthroat?" Frederick asked as he pushed off from the water's edge.

"I don't know, young Frederick, but we better avoid it at all costs," Yellowthroat said.

Frederick and Yellowthroat had lost count of the days they had been carried by the river. Moons had come and gone, new lands seen and faded away, but when they came upon golden sand, Yellowthroat knew they were close.

"What do you see?" Frederick shouted to Yellowthroat who was watching attentively from the bow. Before Yellowthroat could answer, the boat stopped abruptly and flung Frederick headfirst past the bird and over the bow. He landed as softly as one could on yellow sand.

"I see sand," Yellowthroat replied, better late than never.

"Yeah, well, I taste it," Freddie answered, wiping his sleeve across his mouth. "Yuck!" Freddie picked himself up to witness the river dry up, leaving them and the worn boat behind.

"Where are we, Yellowthroat?" Freddie asked, almost fearful of the answer.

"Right where we need to be: Redback Valley. This is a land where every grain of sand begs for water, a land where the sun is too close and the moon too far. This, young Frederick … this is where we'll find the creature who will lead us to the girl with two colored eyes in The Great Blue. Then we can give her Tug's egg."

Freddie grabbed the satchel, patted his pocket to ensure the egg was there, and together he and the bird headed toward the sun.

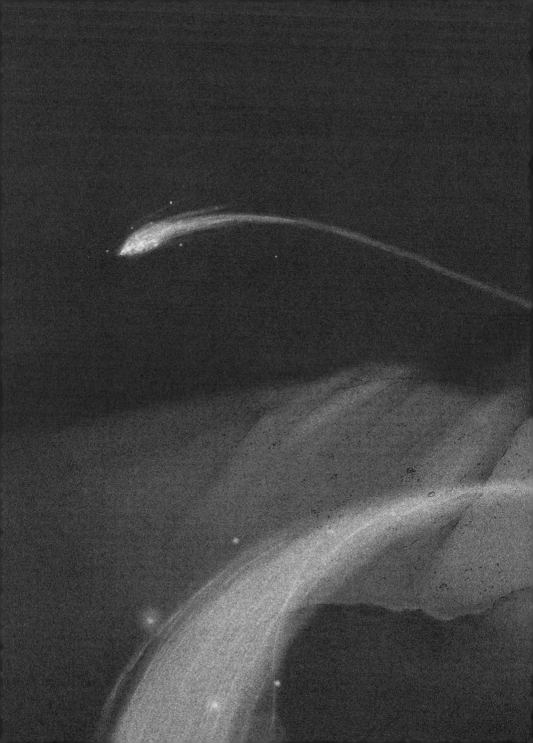

The daytime heat was almost too much to bear, while at night the cold numbed Freddie's toes and the tip of his nose. And like every evening before, Frederick would quietly fall asleep with fresh tears in his eyes, scared and unsure of all that was asked of him.

"Young Frederick, have you ever heard the fable of the pebble's wish?" Yellowthroat asked, sensing his worry.

"Story goes that a lone pebble would stare up high into the heavens each and every day, watching the tips of the great oaks sway and blow. And each and every day this small pebble would dream of being as magnificent as the oaks. One day, a farmhand came along and snatched up the pebble from the hard ground and put it deep in soft, wet dirt. The pebble was confused, sad, and concerned.

"But little did that pebble know that it would soon start to sprout! Vivid green leaves and unforeseen root growth began to form. For this pebble was not a pebble at all but an acorn.

"Don't you see, young Frederick? You thought you were a pebble, but you are really an acorn. And this is your time to grow in the soil and become strong like the oaks. Now get some sleep, for tomorrow we face great hardship."

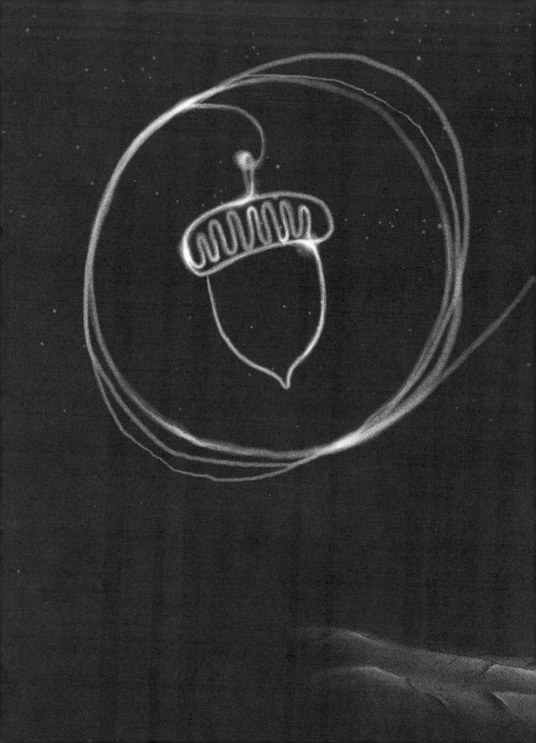

The next morning Frederick woke at first light. *It's colder than usual this morning*, Freddie thought. It was the kind of morning when the sky slowly turns from white to blue. The kind of morning that starts off cold but will quickly turn warm. *The type of morning to forget one's troubles and go fishing.* Freddie smiled to himself, knowing the impossibility of such a thing.

Sitting up in his sandy bed, his thoughts were interrupted by the sound of loud chomping and chewing. Freddie jumped up as quick as a field mouse to see what could possibly be making such a disgusting noise. And then he saw it …

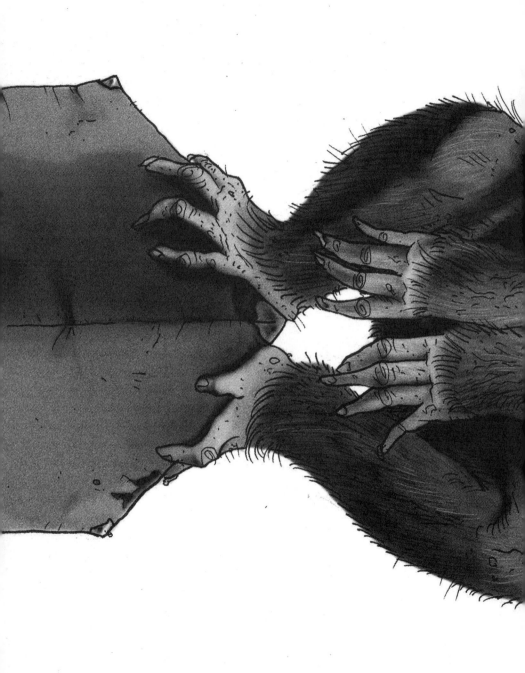

There was a large chimpanzee, squatting with his hand-like feet on top of an old burgundy trunk. Little did Yellowthroat and Frederick know that this mysterious creature had come upon them in the night. His skin was oily, his hair greasy, and his teeth brown as he gnawed the last of their plums from Gloom.

"Yellowthroat, wake up," Frederick said quietly.

"I see it, young Frederick. This is the creature we needed to find, but low and behold it found us. As you can see, he is an unnatural, perplexing, hideous beast. Everyone seeking entrance to The Great Blue is allowed to ask this creature three questions and three questions only. And for every question, one must offer it a treasure. If it likes the prize, then it will give the answer. Do you understand how crucial this is?" Yellowthroat said.

"What's your name?" Frederick nervously yelled to the ape, interrupting Yellowthroat.

"No, Frederick!" Yellowthroat shouted. "Now that will be your first question!"

The ape adjusted its bowler hat then stuck out its long-fingered hands, gesturing for payment.

Yellowthroat sighed.

Frederick removed Tug's book from his satchel and quickly handed the bag over. The chimp snatched it from Freddie's hand and studied the satchel. It touched and sniffed every stitch, pocket, and strap. Then, happy with its new toy, the creature grabbed a small piece of chalk from behind its ear and began to write on the weathered chalkboard hanging around its neck.

It finished writing, then let the chalkboard dangle as before. The words were upside down and barely legible.

"Secret," Yellowthroat read, tilting his head upside down. "The chimp's name is Secret."

Frederick, overcome with the thought that this animal might know all the answers to his questions, quickly blurted out, "Secret, do you know where The Great Blue is?"

Another sigh from Yellowthroat. "I already told you …"

Secret stuck out its hand as before. Freddie looked around their campsite and saw the lantern propped up in the sand. He quickly handed it to Secret.

Secret grabbed the lantern, gave it a couple of licks, then wiped its name from the chalkboard and replaced it with an answer: "Yes."

"Frederick," Yellowthroat said, "the next question is very import—"

"Where is it?!" Frederick blurted, not listening to Yellowthroat.

"Frederick! That was our third and final question!" Yellowthroat cried.

Secret gave a menacing grin and stared at Frederick. Its hands again went palm up. Freddie was holding only one object—the book from Tug. Freddie tried to stare back, but soon gave in and looked down at the sand. There was something about Secret's eyes that made him very uncomfortable.

"Now slow down, Frederick. We can't lose that book," Yellowthroat said.

Freddie peered hard at Secret's empty hand, then gently and regrettably laid the book in it.

Like lightning, the chimp seized the book, and as it glared into Freddie's eyes, it began to tear pages from the binding. With each hot burst of desert wind, another page flew across the sand.

The only thing that stopped remorseful tears from falling down Freddie's cheeks was the screeching sound of Secret's chalk. Secret had drawn an arrow pointing straight up. Freddie immediately looked up at the yellow sky, his eyes squinting and nearly blinded by the searing white sun.

"I don't see anything! What are we looking for?" Frederick cried.

Yellowthroat flew in close to examine the chalkboard. "Frederick, remember every other answer? They were all upside down. The arrow is not pointing up, but down! It's pointing down! The Great Blue must be below us. We are to dig, Frederick! Dig!"

Frederick fell to his knees and began dragging away the sand directly at the ape's feet.

Secret didn't budge; he just watched uninterestedly.

Frederick dug without any regard of when to stop or what might be on the other side. Little Yellowthroat did what he could with every grain of sand.

The two of them dug All day.

And they dug all night.

When Frederick finally stopped to look up, they had dug a hole so deep, he couldn't get out even if he wanted to. The problem, of course, with digging such a deep hole is that there is no longer anywhere to put the dirt once it's been dug. Freddie checked his pocket periodically to make sure the egg was still there, knowing if he were to lose it the mission would be pointless. Then he had an idea … "What if we just use the egg to bring us to The Great Blue?"

"It won't work, young Frederick. Each egg is specific, for each child. Its power wouldn't work even if you tried. Now, fill up your shoes," Yellowthroat said. Frederick did as he was told. When each shoe was full, Yellowthroat took the laces in his beak and carried them up and out of the hole.

For five long days, Frederick and Yellowthroat dug.

But it was on the evening of the fifth day, as the sun was sinking into the horizon, that Freddie finally stopped. "No more, Yellowthroat. I … I just can't," Freddie whispered, resting his head against the cold walls of the deep, sandy pit. "How do we know if this is even right? Tug's book is scattered across the valley. We're in the middle of nowhere … and I'm done," Frederick said.

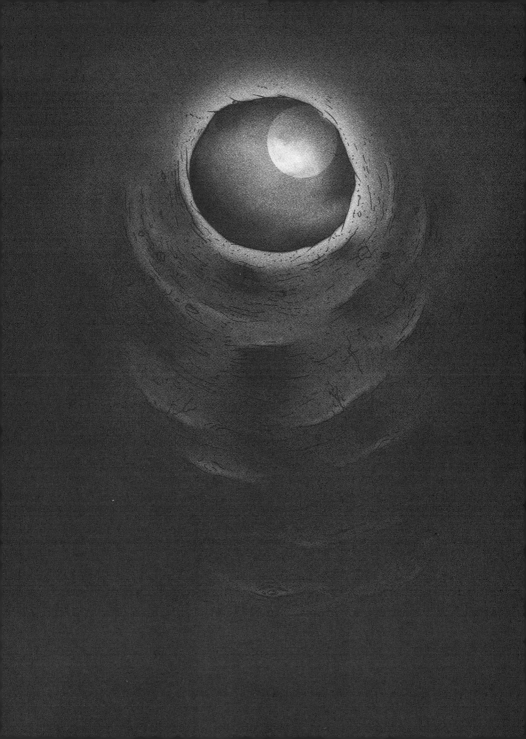

Tears began to roll down his dust-covered cheeks and fall into the sand.

Yellowthroat landed on Freddie's shoulder to comfort the boy but was distracted by something above. "Frederick … look," he said, staring at the rim of the hole.

Freddie glanced up and saw a single piece of paper floating down into the hole like a feather on a windy day. Yellowthroat flew to grab it and bring it close to Frederick. It was torn and dirty, but Frederick knew it was a page from Tug's book.

And right before his very eyes, black ink filled the page…

And Frederick, now
Filled with Hope,
Dug Just a Few
More Inches.

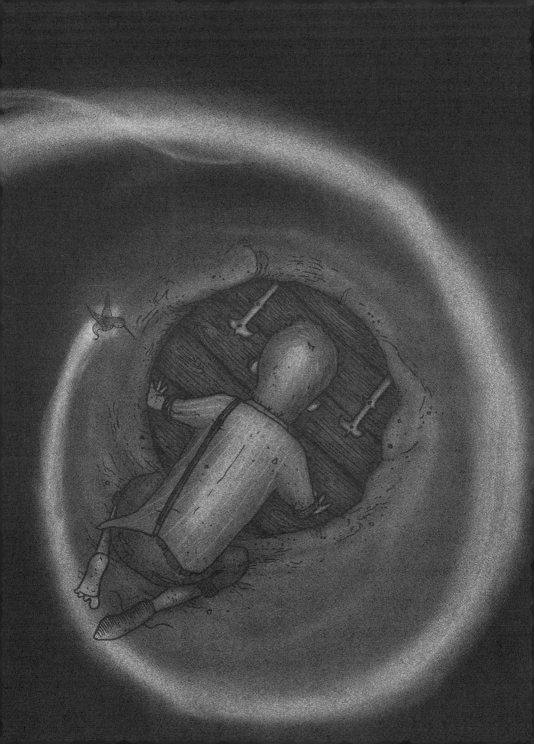

Freddie fell to his knees and brushed away the remaining inches of sand. Yellowthroat's eyes went wide seeing what was before them. Frederick, for the first time in days, smiled with anticipation.

Frederick and Yellowthroat's jaws dropped as the object of their long search became visible. Freddie knew this was it from its shiny egg-shaped doorknob.

"Can you believe it, Yellowthroat? We found it," Freddie whispered as he reached for the handle.

"Open it quickly, young Frederick," Yellowthroat said.

But …

Just then …

The doorknob began to turn … from the other side …

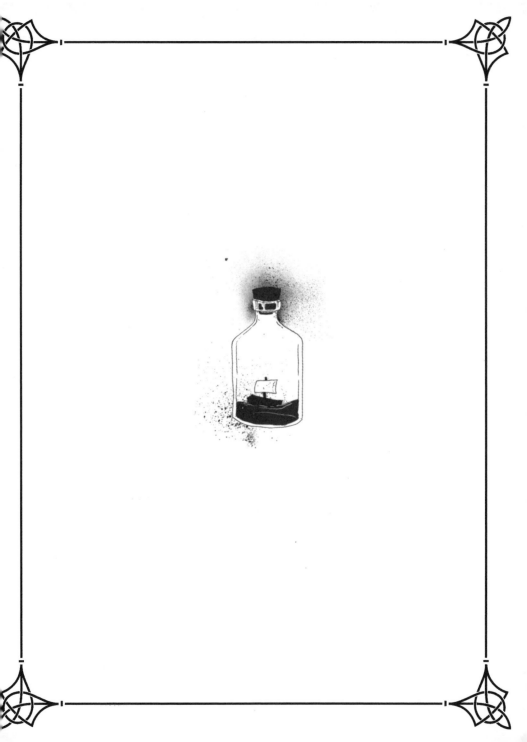